Dear mouse friends,
Welcome to the world of

Geronimo Stilton

THE RODENT'S GAZETTE
EDITORIAL STAFF

Geronimo Stilton
A learned and brainy
mouse; editor of
The Rodent's Gazette

Thea Stilton
Geronimo's sister and
special correspondent at
The Rodent's Gazette

Trap Stilton
An awful joker;
Geronimo's cousin and
owner of the store
Cheap Junk for Less

Benjamin Stilton
A sweet and loving
nine-year-old
mouse; Geronimo's
favorite nephew

Stilton

THE HUNT FOR THE
CURIOUS CHEESE

PLUS a bonus
Mini Mystery and
cheesy jokes!

Scholastic Inc.

ISBN 978-0-545-79151-9

Pages i–111; 194–214 copyright © 2014 by Edizioni Piemme S.p.A., Corso Como 15, 20154 Milan, Italy.

Pages 112–193 copyright © 2007 by Edizioni Piemme S.p.A.

International Rights © Atlantyca S.p.A.

Pages i–111; 194–214 English translation © 2015 by Atlantyca S.p.A.

Pages 112–193 English translation © 2012 by Atlantyca S.p.A.

Based on an original idea by Elisabetta Dami.
www.geronimostilton.com

Published by Scholastic Inc., 557 Broadway, New York, NY 10012.

Pages 1–111
Text by Geronimo Stilton
Original title *Lo strano caso dei formaggi strapuzzoni*
Cover by Francesco Castelli
Illustrations by Silvia Bigolin, Maria De Filippo, and Claudio Cernuschi (concept); Alessandro Muscillo (design); Riccardo Sisti (inks); and Daria Cerchi (color)
Graphics by Paolo Zadra and Chiara Cebraro

Pages 112–193
Text by Geronimo Stilton
Original title *Il topo falsario*
Illustrations by Claudio Cernuschi (pencils and ink) and Giuseppe Di Dio (color)
Graphics by Michela Battaglin
Fingerprint graphic © NREY/Shutterstock

Special thanks to Kathryn Cristaldi and AnnMarie Anderson
Translated by Lidia Morson Tramontozzi and Julia Heim
Interior design by Kay Petronio and Becky James

12 11 10 9 8 7 6 5 4 3 2 1   15 16 17 18 19/0

Printed in Singapore 46

First edition, April 2015

TABLE OF CONTENTS

THE HUNT FOR THE CURIOUS CHEESE

FREE CHEESE TASTING

It was a windy afternoon in February. I was sitting in my office when I **smelled** something in the air. Intrigued, I sniffed again. Yep . . . it was the wonderful aroma of **cheese**!

Oops, sorry, I haven't introduced myself. My name is Stilton, *Geronimo Stilton*! I run *The Rodent's Gazette*, the most famouse newspaper on Mouse Island. Anyway, where was I? Oh, yes. I decided to follow that **delicious** scent of cheese . . .

What a wonderful scent!

I scurried past Singing Stone Square and down Rocky Rat Road. The SCENT of cheese was becoming more and more intense. The cheese was near. I could feel it! I turned the corner and almost ran smack into what looked like a basement door. I read the **SIGN**:

FREE CHEESE TASTING. FIRST COME, FIRST SERVED.

Head down the stairs for some sweet cheesy samples!

By now, I'm embarrassed to say, I was practically DROOLING all over myself. Yes, if there's one thing I cannot resist, it's whisker-licking-good cheese!

I scampered down the stairs and found myself in a dark, dingy cellar with crumbling walls. In the middle of the cellar, there was a table with a million different kinds of cheeses on it (well, okay, maybe not a million, but there were a lot). Next to the table there was a sign that read: **Surprise Sample**. Next to it was a gigantic wedge of cheese.

Puzzled, I scratched my whiskers. What was a **Surprise Sample**? I had no idea, but I wasn't going to worry about it because I was currently overwhelmed by the scent of my favorite treat in the world . . . **cheese**! I grabbed a fork and a dish and headed straight for the table.

But just as I was approaching the table I thought I heard someone giggling. "Hee, hee, hee!"

I **whirled** around. Was someone watching my every pawstep? No, there was no one in sight. I took another step, and then it happened. As I passed the giant wedge of cheese, it grabbed me!

"**Surprise!** Bet you didn't expect the cheese to catch the mouse!" a voice called out.

"Heeeeeeeelp!" I squeaked, my heart hammering. I felt like I was starring in the terrifying horror movie *Revenge of the Rodent-Chomping Cheese Chunks*!

I was about to FAINT from fear when

the giant wedge of cheese began laughing **hysterically**. How odd!

Suddenly, I spotted something else that was odd. A tail was sticking out of the cheese! Then a little door in it snapped open and a mouse with **GRAY** fur and a yellow trench coat peeked out.

"How did you like my little **joke**, Stilton?" the mouse squeaked.

It was my friend **Hercule Poirat**, the famous detective! I should have known. Hercule was always *playing* weird pranks on me and loved to surprise me.

"Very funny," I muttered. Then I braced myself. Every time Hercule surprises me, he wants me to get involved in one of his crazy cases.

"Stilton, I need a little help solving a strange mystery that involves . . . **cheese**!" my friend said.

See what I mean?

THE BANANACYCLE

I tried to make an excuse, but before I knew it, I had agreed to help, starting later that day, and Hercule sped off on his *yellow* bananacycle. **RATS!**

FLEAS MAKE THE BEST FRIENDS!

An hour later I arrived at the door of Hercule's office and **KNOCKED**.

"It's me, Geronimo Stilton!" I squeaked.

As I waited for the door to open, a pile of rancid cheese rinds **WHACKED** me on the head. Chuckling, Hercule poked his head out and let me in.

"What do you think about my **antitheft device**, Stilton? I'll be able to track down any thief who gets hit by these stinky cheese rinds — I'll just follow the **stench**!" He laughed. "I wouldn't want to get hit with those myself."

"But I told you it was me!" I protested.

Hercule grinned. "Yes, but what if it wasn't

you, Stilton? What if it was someone just **pretending** to be you?" he squeaked.

I **rolled** my eyes. Sometimes there's no arguing with Hercule. Now he invited me into his **flea-infested** office. And when I say **flea-infested**, I'm not joking! Hercule just **loves** fleas, and he lives with a ton of them. They camp out on his living room rug and relax on his couch. He even has a pillow that reads, "Fleas make the best friends!"

Right then he called out, "Felicity! Little Felicity!"

A **FLEA** came **BOUNCING** toward him.

"Hi there, Felicity! Here's a little snack!" Hercule said,

BOING!
BOING!

giving her a cookie crumb. He looked over at me and explained, "I'm training her to bring

me my SLIPPERS. Isn't that great?"

Did I mention Hercule is a little, well, strange? "How do you recognize every flea?" I asked.

"By the hairstyle, of course," Hercule explained.

He gave me a MAGNIFYING GLASS and pointed to a group of fleas. "Fifi has little braids, Fiona has red hair, Farrah has curls . . ."

HERCULE'S SLIPPERS

After a while I stopped paying attention. There's only so long a rational rodent can listen to a description of fleas and their hairstyles!

While Hercule BABBLED on and on about his flea hairstyles I edged over toward a yellow pawchair with a blue BANANA pattern. Besides fleas, Hercule loves bananas! But

just as I sank down into the chair . . .

"Ouuuuuuuuuuuuuuuuuch!"

I screeched.

"**Cheese sticks!** So that's what happened to my cactus plant!" Hercule squeaked. "I was wondering where I put it. My cousin **Bloomertail** gave it to me. He's a **florist** and knows all about plants. He says cacti are . . ."

I groaned as he babbled on. I didn't know which was worse — an hour-long story about **fleas**, or one about cacti!

"**Hercule!**" I finally interrupted him, exasperated. "Will you **PLEASE** tell me why you need me?"

A Taste
of Cheese

With a **mysterious** look, Hercule took two identical pieces of cheese out of his safe. He **TASTED** a little piece first from one, then the other, muttering, "Hmm. As I **suspected**." Then he handed me a fork.

"**TASTE** them and tell me what you think."

I tasted both cheeses, one after the other.

They look the same!

"They have the same color, the same consistency, the same aroma, the same taste, and the same label. In other words, they're identical," I said.

He shook his head. "They look identical . . . but they aren't!"

He pulled the label off one of the pieces and inspected it under the microscope.

"Under the microscope, you can see the DIFFERENCES between these labels. One is a copy! The INGREDIENTS in this piece of cheese are not the same as the INGREDIENTS in the other one. It doesn't even have milk in it! In other words, this cheese isn't really cheese . . . it's FAKE!"

I blinked, and he continued. "Someone's making fake cheese and selling it for cheap. If they keep it up, it will put dairy farms out of business!"

"That's terrible!" I squeaked.

"That's why I need your help!" Hercule replied.

I quickly said yes. After all, it would be great to get the scoop for *The Rodent's Gazette.*

"Pick you up tomorrow **MORNING** — we're going to hunt for the curious cheese!" Hercule grinned.

Hmm!

YOU'VE GOT GREEN WARTS!

The following morning I woke up with a **TERRIBLE** itch all over my body. As I scratched, I listened to the news on TV.

"All the cheese factories near New Mouse City are **SHUTTING** down," the announcer said. "It seems that someone has been producing **COUNTERFEIT** cheeses and putting everyone else out of business!"

Right then there was a knock at my front door. Hercule stood outside. "Come on, Stilton, we've got to get cracking on our hunt. Hop in the **bananamobile**!"

Yep, Hercule loves **BANANAS** so much that even his car is shaped like one!

"I thought we could drive around and

VROOOOOOM!

look for **cheesy clues**," Hercule squeaked.

I was about to ask what a cheesy clue would look like when my friend pointed at my snout.

"Do you know you have a huge green wart on your nose?" he asked.

I looked in the rearview MIRROR. Rancid rat hairs! It was true!

Then I looked at Hercule. "You've got green warts, too!" I squeaked.

Right then, I got an attack of the hiccups. **"HIC! HIC! HIC! HIC!"**

Then Hercule started burping.

BURP!! BURP! BURP!

A second later my stomach began to ache and gurgle.

GURGLE!

GURGLE! GURGLE!

I've gotta run to the bathroom!

Ugh!

I looked at **Hercule** and saw he was clutching his stomach, too.

Right then we both shouted at the same time, "I've gotta run to the bathroom! Now! Quick! ASAP!"

Luckily, we were right by my office, so we screeched to a stop. We ran through *The Rodent's Gazette* building, screaming at everyone in our path.

"MOOOOOOOOOOOOOOOOOOOOVE!"

"GET OUT OF THE WAAAAAAAY!"

"INCOMIIIIIIIIIIIIIIIIIIIING!"

After I came out of the bathroom, Kreamy O'Cheddar, editor in chief of *The Rodent's Gazette*, ran up to me, looking worried.

"It happened to you, too, Mr. Stilton? I've had a STOMACHACHE for a week," she confided.

Merenguita Gingermouse put a little POWDER on her nose and said, "And I've been sprouting green warts all week!"

"Me, too!" Zeppola Zap agreed. "I look like I'm dressed as a witch for Halloween!"

Even my cousin Trap, who never gets rattled about anything, was upset. "Last night I ate some fondue," he said. "Ever since then, I've done nothing but run to the bathroom . . ."

He suddenly scurried away at full speed, waving a roll of **toilet paper**.

"Gotta go!" he called.

Great chunks of cheddar! This situation was not good.

At that moment an alert came

on the computer screen in my office. It seemed that New Mouse City's **emergency** room was packed with rodents all experiencing symptoms of food poisoning — including peculiar green warts!

Can We Come to Your House?

Before I could finish reading the alert, **FLIP HOTPAWS** burst into the room. Flip owns the local diner. Right now he was carrying enough food to feed an **ARMY** of rodents! *"What's going on?"* I asked, surprised.

FLIP HOTPAWS

PINKY PICK, my assistant editor, was astonished. "Boss, don't you remember? Benjamin, Bugsy Wugsy, and all of their **classmates** are coming into the office today!" she squeaked.

I smacked a **paw** on my forehead.

Of course! Today was the day of their field trip to *The Rodent's Gazette*! Every year, elementary school teacher **Miss Angel Paws** organized a field trip to the paper to show her students how a daily paper is born.

I was just telling Hercule that our **FAKE** cheese investigation would have to wait, when suddenly the building was invaded by a group of mouselets snapping **photos** and **DRiLLiNG** me with questions.

"*Mr. Stilton*, is it true you've been doing this job since you were in diapers?"

"*Mr. Stilton*, do you have a girlfriend?"

"*Mr. Stilton,* can we come over to your house?"

Blistering blue cheese! What a curious group of little mice. All of their questions were making me **dizzy**.

Finally, I suggested we take a break to try Flip Hotpaws's cheesy treats.

Soon the mouselets were stuffing their snouts with cheese pastries. The only one

Some cheese?

No, thank you!

not eating was Miss Angel Paws, who was **ALLERGIC** to cheese.

"Interesting!" I exclaimed. "You're the only one who doesn't have green warts . . ."

"There's a mystery to be **SOLVED** here, Stilton," Hercule agreed.

But before we could discuss anything, my stomach began to **GURGLE** up a storm. It was so **LOUD**, I could barely hear myself squeak!

"Sorry, I forgot something at home," I mumbled to Miss Angel Paws, clutching my stomach and racing for the door.

How **embarrassing**!

THE BANANACAMPER IS WAITING!

The next **morning**, Hercule arrived at my house. To our surprise, **Benjamin** and *Bugsy Wugsy* came running up.

"We want to help!" Benjamin said.

"We know you're on a **mysterious** hunt involving the fake cheese. Can we help you, Uncle G?" Bugsy squeaked. "Can we?"

Now let me just say, Bugsy can **DRiVe** any mouse up a clock! But she is Benjamin's friend, and I have a hard time saying **no** to my sweet nephew.

"Guess what, **UNCLE**? We already searched the Internet and found out lots of **INFORMATION** on the case," Benjamin said. "Listen to this . . ."

BENJAMIN AND BUGSY WUGSY'S FINDINGS

1. In the Ravingrat Ravine, southwest of New Mouse City, someone just built an enormous factory of food products, named Furever Foods.

WHO?

2. The factory was built in only one night.

HOW?

3. Within the last week, a stream of trucks has been leaving the factory, heading . . .

WHERE?

4. Mysterious machinery has been delivered to the factory, and the whole place is gated off with barbed wire so no one can get in.

WHY?

5. Within the past week, every rodent who has eaten cheese is covered with green warts. Only those who haven't eaten any cheese (like Miss Angel Paws) don't have warts.

"Wow, what **GREAT** information!" I said after Benjamin finished. "You two really know how to research."

"So what do we do now?" asked Bugsy Wugsy.

"We have to go check out that mysterious factory in **RAVINGRAT RAVINE**!" Hercule exclaimed.

"Can we come with you?" **Benjamin** asked excitedly.

Let us come, Uncle G!

Well . . .

"Well, I don't know . . . it might be **dangerous**," I said, worried.

But Hercule wasn't concerned. "Sure!" he said, **WAVING** us down the block. "The more the **merrier**. But enough **SQUEAKING**! Let's hit the road. The **bananacamper** is waiting for us."

Have you ever seen Hercule Poirat's **bananacamper**? It's a pretty incredible means of transportation. It looks just like you might expect it to. It's basically a **SUPERLONG**, supermodern house on wheels. Oh, and of course, it's in the shape of a **banana**!

Inside the camper, Hercule pulled out two **TINY** stereo speakers and sat them on the dashboard. "These are solar powered," he explained.

HERCULE'S BANANACAMPER

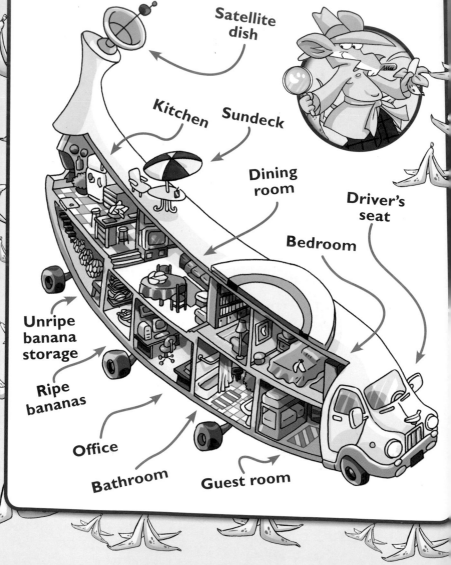

Satellite dish

Kitchen

Sundeck

Dining room

Driver's seat

Bedroom

Unripe banana storage

Ripe bananas

Office

Bathroom

Guest room

Then he began **blasting** music so loud my ears began ringing.

I Don't Like Beans!

As soon as we arrived in **RaViNGRat RaViNe**, our camper filled with a disgusting **stench**.

"Stilton, did you have **beans** for breakfast?" Hercule accused me.

Yuck!

"It wasn't me!" I protested. "I thought it was you!"

Hercule looked **offended**.

"For your **INFORMATION**, I don't even like beans . . ." he began.

He was interrupted by Benjamin, who had lowered a window. "Hey, everyone, the smell is coming from outside — from the factory!" he squeaked, **wrinkling** his nose.

Hercule took a pair of binoculars from his pocket and passed them to me.

"Take a peek, Stilton," he suggested.

So I did. I saw an **IMMENSE** building, made of wood and cement, surrounded by **HIGH** walls that were protected by barbed wire. On top of the factory, there was a **CLOUD** of stinky black smoke. Weird!

"What an **ODD-LOOKING** food factory," Bugsy observed.

As we sat watching, a steady file of **GRAY** trucks entered and left the factory. At the entrance gate, they all pressed a special code into a keypad.

"*Twisted rat tails!* I wonder what those trucks are carrying," Hercule muttered.

The road was **BLOCKED** by a checkpoint with a sign that read:

THIS FACTORY IS POLLUTED!

We decided to camp out in a WOODED area near the factory to see if we could find out what was going on. The first thing I noticed was that all of the plants near the factory had turned yellow. The grass under my paws was dry, and a stream running in the woods was a sickly orange color.

Holey cheese!

"This factory is polluting the environment!" cried Benjamin indignantly.

Night had fallen on stinky RaVINGrat RaViNe, but the trucks continued to come and go. The factory was now lit by

neon lights that **ILLUMINATED** the area like daylight. We gathered around the campfire to figure out our next move.

"Okay, so I think we need to find a way to get into that **factory**. Then we can see what they are producing there, and we can document all of the ways they are *polluting* the area," Hercule proposed.

As the campfire BURNED into the night we came up with a STEP-BY-STEP plan. Bugsy Wugsy wrote it all down,

Let's make a plan . . .

then read the plan out loud:

 1 HERCULE AND GERONIMO WILL SNEAK INTO THE FACTORY AND LOOK FOR CLUES.

2 BENJAMIN AND BUGSY WILL HIDE OUT NEARBY.

3 HERCULE AND GERONIMO WILL KEEP IN CONTACT WITH THE MOUSELETS VIA CELL PHONE.

4 HERCULE AND GERONIMO WILL COMMUNICATE THEIR FINDINGS TO THE MOUSELETS, WHO WILL RESEARCH THEM ONLINE IN THE CAMPER.

5 IF BENJAMIN AND BUGSY LOSE CONTACT WITH GERONIMO AND HERCULE, THEY WILL CALL FOR HELP!

"Hmm. There's only one problem with the plan," Hercule noted. "How do we sneak into the factory? The bananacamper doesn't exactly look like those GRAY delivery trucks."

"I know what we can do. We'll put **mud** all over the camper. You'll **BLEND** right in with the trucks!" Benjamin suggested.

"Mud on my gorgeous bananacamper?" Hercule squeaked with a sob. "My heart is *breaking*!"

Hmmm . . .

"But even if no one recognizes us, don't we need to know the **secret code** to get in?" I asked, worried.

Bugsy giggled. "We're **two** steps ahead of you, Uncle G!" she announced. "Benjamin

and I used the camera's **ZOOM** lens to film the truckers **PUNCHING** in the code!"

"Great work!" Hercule exclaimed. "I have another idea. Just in case anyone eavesdrops, we should each have a code name. I will be **Banana One**. Geronimo, you can be **Banana Two**, and you mouselets will be **Banana Three**!"

HERE'S THE CAMOUFLAGED BANANACAMPER!

He grabbed his cell phone and began babbling. "**Banana One** to **Banana Two**. Do you read me? Do you read me?"

Even though I was standing right next to Hercule, he wouldn't stop asking until I screamed, "Yes! Yes, I read you, **Banana One**!" Hercule loves playing **secret agent**.

We **splattered** the camper with mud and took off. Benjamin and Bugsy called after us. "Good luck!"

Moldy mozzarella, we would need it!

96 — MY GRANNY'S AGE!

Before long we reached the gate. The truck driver in front of us tapped in the code. Then the gate locked behind him.

96 MY GRANNY IRONWHISKERS'S AGE!

"**Banana Two** to **Banana Three**," I whispered into my phone. "Would you please give me the **secret code** to open the gate?"

A minute later I heard Bugsy Wugsy's voice loud and clear

4 THE NUMBER OF MINUTES I LIKE MY EGGS TO BE BOILED!

2 THE NUMBER OF SECONDS SINCE I THOUGHT ABOUT YOUR SISTER!

35 THE NUMBER OF DAYS UNTIL YOUR SISTER'S BIRTHDAY!

at the other end. "**Code?** What **code**?" she squeaked.

I **froze**. What? Didn't she have the code? Luckily, a moment later, Bugsy read off a series of numbers. I should have known — Bugsy loves to **PULL** my paw!

But right then my cell reception cut out.

"**Cheese and crackers!**" I wailed to Hercule. "I don't remember the numbers Bugsy told me!"

"Calm down, Stilton! I heard Bugsy and **remember** every number perfectly!" Hercule insisted. Here's how . . ."

8 THE NUMBER OF WHEELS ON MY CAMPER!

11 THE NUMBER OF BANANAS ON MY TABLE AT HOME!

3 THE NUMBER OF GREEN WARTS I HAVE ON MY NOSE!

Behind us, truck drivers began **honking**. Oh, what a **NIGHTMARE**!

But then Hercule pressed in the code: 3-11-8-35-2-4-96. The gate to Furever Foods Factory opened. The bananacamper was in!

One of the guards directed us to a parking spot, then approached the camper and remarked, "How come your truck is **different** from the others?"

"Uh, this is the latest model," Hercule sputtered.

When the guard looked **skeptical**, Hercule added, "Why be ordinary when you can be **EXTRAORDINARY**!"

I thought that last bit was over the top (Hercule is so

dramatic!), but the guard didn't blink.

"Okay, whatever you say, buddy. Just let me know how many mice you'll need to help you unload," he said.

I GULPED. Unload the camper? **CURDLED CREAM CHEESE!** Now we'd be found out!

But Hercule didn't flinch. "Help?" he scoffed. "We don't need help. We may look SCRAWNY, but my friend and I are former **PUMPING PAWS BODY BUILDERS**. We can unload this delivery in a flash! We'll be fine on our own."

Again, the guard looked **SKEPTICAL**. Luckily, just then, another truck needed help unloading, so he waved us on.

FAKE CHEESE OUT OF ROTTEN GARBAGE!

As soon as the guard was out of sight, we **raced** over to the factory and slipped inside. In front of us was a long flight of stairs. We climbed until I began to feel *dizzy*. Did I mention I'm afraid of heights?

When we reached the top I realized we were at the **ceiling** of the factory's largest room!

"Let's climb along the beam. We can check things out without being seen," Hercule suggested.

I **slid** along the beam with my eyes closed.

Oh, how do I get myself in these TERRIFYING situations?!

"Don't be a **coward**, Stilton! Open your eyes!" Hercule insisted. So I did . . .

What an incredible sight!

Below us thousands of workers were **creating** the curious cheese. They were pushing carts filled with **moldy** cheese rinds — and worms, dirt, and other **stinky** garbage. All of that was thrown into a huge pot and boiled. The mixture was then treated with a **CHEMICAL** substance that gave it the flavor of different types of real cheese, like mozzarella or cheddar. Finally, the fake cheese was cut into pieces and painted **yellow**.

Some workers made HOLES in the fake cheese; others painted it with spray guns for special color effects. Others put fake cheese in the oven to smoke it. Still others made FAKE LABELS that looked just like real cheese labels, which were then pasted onto the fake cheese.

"Can you believe these CROOKS?" grumbled Hercule. "They are making fake cheese out of rotten garbage! Wait till my granny Ironwhiskers hears about this! Her whiskers will whirl with outrage! Her fur will stand on end . . ."

Have you ever met Granny Ironwhiskers Poirat? Let's just say, she is one TOUGH rodent!

Hercule suddenly turned to me. "Did Thea eat any cheese? Is she covered in green warts? Oooohhh, I hope not! They would clash with her beautiful VIOLET eyes!" he squeaked.

I rolled my eyes. Hercule has a **major crush** on my sister!

Hercule was still squeaking away when we spotted two guards below us WHiSPeRiN8 together. We eavesdropped on their conversation . . .

"I'm bringing the **BOSS** a little broth that's good for settling the stomach," one of the guards said.

"Did you see how many **warts** the boss has?" the other said.

"Yeah, it's because the boss is always munching on the **disgusting** fake cheese we're producing!" the first guard replied.

"I know. But don't say anything about it in there. You know all about the boss's **TERRIBLE** temper," the other added.

Carefully, we **slid** down the beam and followed the guards to a heavy door. They *rang* a bell, then said the password: "Rotten to the core!"

The door silently opened, revealing a **LARGE** shape wearing a big WHITE apron. In the background, we could see an office.

EVEN ICE CREAM!

The guards left just as the phone rang. *What luck!* As the large rodent went to answer it, we slipped inside and hid.

"Yes, Sleezer. All the rodents in New Mouse City ate my cheese — that's why they all have **green warts**. Oh, except for that teacher, Angel Paws. But who cares! Now that I know my formula works, I can make all kinds of fake foods . . . like **pasta**, **JELLY**, **chocolate** . . . even ice cream!"

Now I was worried. **VeRRRRY** worried. This **ROTTEN** rodent was working with Sleezer!

Do you know about Sleezer? He's a **mysterious** sewer rat who's out to take over New Mouse City!

"My fake foods will be so cheap, everyone will buy them," the large rodent continued squeaking. "The other food manufacturers will go 𝔹ℝ𝕆𝕂𝔼, and New Mouse City will be mine!"

The rodent coughed.

"Oh, of course, hch-heh. I didn't mean **MINE** — I meant **OURS**, Sleezer. I know it was your idea. Of course — you built the factory in one night. And **PAID** for it all with your money. I was a **NOBODY** when you met me in that stinky restaurant kitchen, and I haven't forgotten . . ."

The rodent rambled on for so long I was afraid I would fall asleep and start **SNORING**. But suddenly my ears perked up. Somehow, the rodent had found out that Hercule, the mouselings, and I were investigating the case.

Holey cheese! They were looking out for us so they could stop our investigation! I began to sweat so much that I thought I might drown in it. I was a nervous wreck!

Meanwhile, the rodent was still blabbing away . . .

"What, Sleezer? You say you accidentally ate the fake cheese and have a green wart on your chin? Ha! Well that just shows you how well I've been able to *imitate* the cheese! But don't worry. I have an ANTIDOTE for it — that is, a medicine that will get rid of the side effects of the poison. No, without the antidote the warts won't go away.

"That's the beauty of my **fake foods**. Everyone will eat them, and then they will have to buy the ANTIDOTE that I will produce. We'll charge a **TON** of money for it! Then I'll be rich! Rich! Rich! Uh, I mean, *we'll* be rich! Rich! Rich! I give you my word — the word of **Viola Vilewhiskers**!"

Viola Vilewhiskers

Who she is: An obnoxious cook who can perfectly imitate any kind of cheese by using garbage scraps.

Who her accomplice is: Sleezer, the evil sewer rat who wants to take over New Mouse City.

Distinguishing marks: A mole on the left side of her snout.

Her secret: She has . . . no, I'm not going to tell you. You'll find out at the end of the story!

Her dream: To control Mouse Island by blackmailing all the inhabitants!

Her weakness: She likes to taste test everything she cooks . . . even her fake foods that cause warts!

3 RIGHT, 1 LEFT, 9 RIGHT . . .

Finally, Viola hung up the phone. A minute later she began scratching her snout like a crazed rat with fleas.

"**Festering furballs!**" she screeched, grabbing a mirror. "I knew I shouldn't have eaten that fake cheddar this morning. I'm covered in green warts!"

Ugh!

Then she sighed. "Oh well, better get the **ANTIDOTE**."

She ran to her safe and entered the combination, muttering the numbers aloud as she did: "Let's see, that's **3** right, **1** left, **9** right, **5** left, and **4** right."

VIOLA'S
ANTIDOTE

Suddenly, she looked around shiftily. "I probably shouldn't say those numbers out loud. Good thing I'm **ALL ALONE**," she quickly consoled herself.

Then she opened the safe and took out a vial filled with a **DARK PURPLE** liquid. She lifted the vial to her mouth and took a long sip.

Within seconds, I saw that her warts were already beginning to DISAPPEAR!

FIVE WATERMELON SEEDS . . .

Viola checked her REFLECTION. Then she left.

"Now what?" I asked Hercule.

But my friend was already **running** for the safe. "I **MEMORIZED** the code, Stilton. Now we break into that safe!" he announced.

The combination?

WE RAN TO THE SAFE, AND HERCULE RECITED THE COMBINATION.

Here's the antidote! I see . . .

WE OPENED THE SAFE. INSIDE WE FOUND THE FORMULA TO MAKE THE ANTIDOTE!

Hercule recited the combination: "**3** right, **1** left, **9** right, **5** left, **4** right . . ."

The safe opened, and we found the **FORMULA** to make the antidote inside!

Just as Hercule finished copying down the **ingredients**, the door to the lab opened. **CHEESE STICKS!** It was Viola Vilewhiskers!

"Catch those **SPIES**!" Viola screeched at her guards.

She grabbed the vial with the antidote, but

Spies!

Run!

Argh!

VIOLA RIPPED THE ANTIDOTE'S FORMULA FROM OUR PAWS . . .

. . . BUT THE PAPER FLEW AWAY AND ENDED UP IN THE FIREPLACE!

ANTIDOTE FOR GREEN WARTS

Combine

- A pinch of baking soda
- A half stick of licorice
- 5 watermelon seeds
- A pinch of nutmeg
- 10 chamomile flowers
- 3 basil leaves
- A small slice of ginger

Then add the **secret ingredient**.

(Sorry. I can't tell you what it is. Otherwise it wouldn't be a **secret**!)

it slipped from her paws and **shattered** into a thousand pieces on the floor. Then she ripped the formula from our paws, but the paper *flew* away and ended up in the fireplace, where there was a lively **FIRE** burning. In the blink of an eye, the recipe was in ashes.

"I worked years and years to find the antidote for green warts, and now it's gone!" Viola sobbed. "Mommy told me to make a copy of the formula, but I didn't listen to her! She was always **nagging** me. 'Comb your fur, Viola! Brush your teeth! Don't play with electronic devices in the bathtub!' **NAG! NAG! NAG!** With a mother like that, it's a wonder I turned out so amazingly **FABUMOUSE**!

"Anyway, where was I? Oh, right — it's all your fault that it's gone now! I'm going to make you two very sorry you ever messed with me, the **bRiLLiaNt** and devious **Viola Vilewhiskers**!"

But before she could grab us, we took off at breakneck speed!

We heard the guards **SHOUTING** and running after us. As we turned a corner, we saw a large **steel door** and went right through it, shutting it quickly behind us.

DARK? YOU THINK IT'S DARK?

I was breathing so heavily, I felt like my lungs would **BURST**! Did I mention I'm not the most *athletic* mouse on the block?

After catching my breath, I looked around. We were in a **dark** warehouse filled with machines that made the CREEPIEST noises . . .

CLICK CLACK!   TICK TICK!

CRUUUUUUNCH!
CRUUUUNCH!
WHIRR! WHIRR!

WHIRR!

BOING!   BOING!
BOING!

"I can't see a thing! It's so **dark**!" I whispered.

"**Dark?** You think it's dark? I can see perfectly clearly!" Hercule bragged.

He turned, **BUMPED** into me, and knocked me against a machine. Ugh!

"Open your eyes, Stilton! It's really not that dark. Then maybe you'll stop **bumping** into things!" Hercule snorted.

"I have eyes like a cat," Poirat went on. As he spoke, he **TRIPPED** over a basket

I can see perfectly!

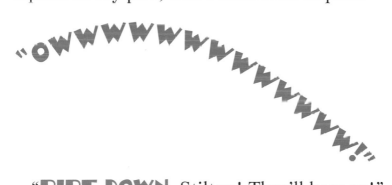

filled with **CEMENT** bricks. The bricks squashed my paw, and I screeched in pain.

"OWWWWWWWWWWWWWW!"

"**PIPE DOWN**, Stilton! They'll hear us!" Hercule scolded.

Stilton . . .   Owww!

Then he turned, **bumping** me so hard that . . . **1** I fell into a huge tub filled with ice cream. *Splash!*

2 I **swam** to the top of the tub and **3** jumped out, but **4** I ended up on a conveyor belt covered with sticky **marshmallow** and crunchy bits of walnuts.

"**HELP!**" I yelled, to no response.

Then **5** I was hit by an **avalanche** of **CANDIED** cherries. **UGH!** At which point **6** Hercule tasted a sample of my coating and squeaked, "Next time do you think you could try rolling around in some **rainbow sprinkles**? I like sprinkles."

My whiskers **shook** with exasperation. Actually, I was also shivering. That ice cream had been so **cold**!

"Hmm, you look like you need to **WARM**

up, Stilton," Hercule observed. He pushed me under a hot-air jet.

Within seconds, everything **melted** off me. A puddle formed around me.

I'm melting . . .

A FLASHLIGHT?

We continued walking through the dark warehouse. "If only we had a flashlight," I sighed.

"I have a flashlight," Hercule replied calmly.

To my shock, he pulled out a flashlight from the **pocket** of his trench coat and passed it to me.

"Why didn't you tell me **EARLIER**?" I sputtered.

"It was much more **ADVENTURESOME** in the dark, don't you think?" he replied, starting to chuckle like a mad mouse.

"**ADVENTURESOME?** Adventuresome, really?" I **FUMED**, willing myself not to **scream** at the top of my lungs.

We turned on the *FLASHLIGHT* and scurried along the halls between one machine and another. It was a labyrinth! After a while, I figured we were lost.

"Hmmm," Hercule muttered, "I don't know if the exit is on the **LEFT** or on the *right*. On the left the hall is wider . . . but, there's more light on the right. On the left we can move along the wall . . . but on the right there's a shortcut. It's **WARMER** on the left . . . but the **stench** is stronger on the right," Hercule mumbled.

One thing you should know about Hercule is that he can never make a decision! At this rate, he'd be blabbering away for hours.

Just then, we heard the sound of footsteps. Stinky Swiss slices! It had to be the guards who had been *CHASING* us earlier.

GERONIMOOOO!

We separated and hid behind two different piles of **BOXES**. Unfortunately, just at that very moment, my cell phone **beeped**!  **RAT-MUNCHING RATTLESNAKES!** I had forgotten to shut it off! I frantically pressed all the buttons and whispered as LㅇW as I could.

"Hello. This is *Geronimo Stilton*."

"Geronimoooo! Where are you? I've been **LOOKING** for you!" my sister, Thea, shrilled.

"**Shhhhh!** Don't shout. I'll tell you everything when I get back. Bye."

But my sister kept squeaking.

BANANACYCLE

"Who were you with the other day? I saw you on a **yellow** motorcycle," she said.

"It's Hercule Poirat's **bananacycle**," I said softly.

"Does he also have a **yellow** convertible? I saw you at the light on Provolone Way," she continued.

"**YES**. That was his **bananamobile**," I added.

"And this morning you were in a **yellow** camper?" she squeaked.

"**YES**! That was the

BANANAMOBILE

BANANACAMPER

BANANACOPTER

BANANAPLANE

bananacamper," I muttered impatiently.

"And Hercule has a **yellow** helicopter and airplane, right?" my sister murmured.

"The **bananacopter** and the **bananaplane**," I squeaked quickly. "Now listen, Thea —"

Here's something to know about my sister: she always has to have the last word. "No, **YOU** listen, Gerrykins," she interrupted.

Tell him . . .

Bye!

"Tell Hercule that on Sunday the Flying Fur Aviation Academy is sponsoring a contest between the two best pilots on Mouse Island. That's right, my **pink** plane against Hercule's **yellow** one!"

"Okay, I'll tell him. Bye!" I squeaked all in one breath, and hung up.

Still, it was too late. The guards had found us. I tried calling Benjamin and Bugsy for help, but Viola appeared and **GRABBED** my phone.

FIVE BELOW ZERO!

The guards grabbed me by the tail. They had also captured Hercule!

"Here, why don't you *relax* and **COOL** down," Viola cackled as the guards pushed us inside an enormouse freezer. The door slammed closed behind us. **Bam!**

It was **cold** in there! The temperature was getting lower and lower. I found a thermometer . . . it was **FIVE BELOW ZERO**! My teeth chattered from cold.

"We b-b-b-better th-th-think of s-s-s-omething f-fast, or we're g-g-g-going to turn into f-f-f-frozen mousicles!" I stammered.

I tried to warm up by jumping **UP** and **DOWN**, but nothing worked. My tail turned **BLUE**. Icicles hung from my whiskers.

Oh, what a way to go!

Headlines flashed before my eyes: *Publisher Freezes in Fridge! Cold Ending to Curious Cheese Case!*

In desperation, Hercule pulled a bunch of tools from his trench coat, including a HAMMER and a **WRENCH**. But the

Brrr!

It's cold!

5 DEGREES BELOW ZERO

door wouldn't budge.

Finally, Hercule pulled something else from his coat. Was it a jackhammer? A crowbar? No, it was only a banana.

I was about to start **SOBBING** when a miracle happened.

I heard voices shouting, "New Mouse City Police!"

"GIVE YOURSELVES UP!"

Funny. The voices sounded familiar . . .

The factory's alarm was blasting, and the freezer door flew open. We saw Viola and her guards fleeing in a **SUBMARINE**.

Then we noticed two mice scampering toward us. Can you guess who they were? **Benjamin and Bugsy!**

"We put Mr. Poirat's speakers outside the gate and made believe the **POLICE** had surrounded the factory," Benjamin explained.

Hercule laughed. "Those speakers were a gift from **GRANNY IRONWHISKERS**. I can't wait to tell her! *They saved us!*"

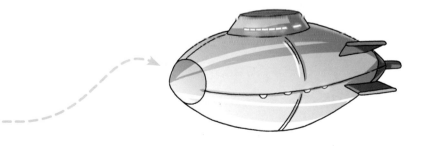

I'LL BE BACK!

As the submarine moved away, we heard Viola **scream**, "I'll be back! And the next time, you'd better **hold** on to your tail! I'll give you more than little green warts! I give you my word — the word of **Viola Vilewhiskers**!"

I shivered. Something told me Viola was a mouse true to her word.

When we got back in the **bananacamper** Hercule cheered, "We did it! We solved the case!"

Soon we were headed back home, with me

in the driver's seat. I was driving for about five minutes when Hercule **SCREAMED** at the top of his lungs, "**STOP!**"

I braked abruptly.

"What is it?" I asked, worried.

He ran out of the camper and pointed to a line of TiNY SNAiLS.

"You almost **RAN** them over!" he cried.

He came back into the camper, and started singing us a song . . .

"I love everything in nature,

from the tiger to the snail.

The sloth, the snake, the glowworm,

the lion, and the whale!

Animals are my friends,

and I respect all forms of life.

I am a vegetarian,

and I try to cause no strife.

Let's all be kind together —

we'll be as happy as can be!

Now let's all eat bananas!

Yum, yum, yum, yum, Yippee!"

Hercule **loves** everything that's environmentally friendly. When he finished his song, he **PULLED** a lever, and four bicycles **popped** up from the floor of the bananacamper.

Huh?

Start pedaling!

Hercule jumped on one of the bikes and shouted, "No sense polluting the air with more gas FUMES. Everyone start pedaling! We'll be back in **NEW MOUSE CITY** in a jiffy!"

CASE CLOSED!

THE HUNT FOR THE CURIOUS CHEESE WAS OVER AND ALL OF THE FAKE CHEESE WAS DESTROYED. HERCULE HAD A COPY OF THE ANTIDOTE FORMULA, AND THE FUREVER FOODS FACTORY WAS USED TO PRODUCE THE ANTIDOTE FOR THE WARTS. IT WAS GIVEN TO EVERYONE FOR FREE.

GOOD-BYE, GREEN WARTS! HELLO, CLEAR FUR!

V. V.

Now, you'd think that's where my story ends. But it's not!

The following day, Hercule invited me to his grandmother's house.

I was happily looking forward to seeing Granny Ironwhiskers.

GRANNY IRONWHISKERS POIRAT

Too bad Hercule insisted we drive there on his bananacycle. We **zoomed** through the city at breakneck speed. Oh, why did he have to drive so fast?

Near the cheese market, we slowed down. And that's when I spotted her. She had **RED** hair and wore a white apron and yellow

slippers embroidered with the initials **V. V.**
She was pushing a cart filled with cheese.
I pointed her out to Hercule who shrieked,
"That's . . . **Viola Vilewhiskers!**"

The rodent was now inches away but didn't
seem to notice us.

HoW StRaNge!

"She's still trying to poison us all!" I
squeaked.

Hercule shouted, "Paws up, Viola
Vilewhiskers! We know it's you!"

For an instant she **STARED** at us,
dumbfounded. Then she laughed.

"Viola? Ha, ha, ha! I'm not Viola! My name
is Victoria."

Hercule and I blinked.

"But . . . you look . . . I mean, your **fur** —
that is, your **slippers** . . ." I stammered.

Victoria sighed and shook her head. "Viola is my **TWIN SISTER**," she explained.

I took a better **look** at her. She was identical to Viola in every way, except her mole was on her right cheek!

"Viola and I look identical, but in reality, we're very different. I love **NATURAL** foods. She likes **artificial** foods. And

LOVES NATURAL FOODS

LOVES ARTIFICIAL FOODS

VICTORIA

Viola

I heard she's mixed up with that rotten rat, Sleezer. If you are looking for her, I'm guessing she's in **TROUBLE** again," Victoria explained.

I nodded. "We had to **shut down** her factory," I squeaked. Then I stuck out my **PAW**. "Excuse me, I forgot to introduce myself. My name is Stilton, *Geronimo Stilton*. I run *The Rodent's Gazette*. Sorry to have bothered you," I added.

"No problem," Victoria said. "In fact, I'd love it if you came to eat at my restaurant. It's called THE NATURAL NIBBLER, and it's on Blue Cheese Boulevard."

We accepted her offer with pleasure. And I must say, the food there was whisker-licking-good!

After we finished eating, Victoria showed us around her kitchen. It was filled with lots

of fresh organic vegetables, WHOLE GRAINS, and fruits. Not a bit of **fake cheese** in sight!

Yep, the two sisters might look identical, but their cooking habits were worlds apart.

Delicious!

THE ABC'S OF HEALTHY EATING

ADDITIVES: Substances that are added to food to change its characteristics, such as color (**dyes**), taste (**flavor**), or storage length (**preservatives**). They can be natural (like herbs) or man-made (like artificial sweeteners).

CARBOHYDRATES: Carbohydrates are basically sugars, and are very important to give our bodies **energy**. They are categorized as simple carbohydrates (**sweeteners**) and complex carbohydrates (**starches**, found in foods like bread, pasta, potatoes, and beans). For a healthy diet, it's important to limit the amount of simple carbohydrates and opt for complex carbohydrates instead.

FATS: The body uses fat as a **fuel** source. Some types of fat can be found in foods such as butter, meat, and fish; other types can be found in processed foods; still other types can be found in oils. However, too much of certain types of fats can be unhealthy.

FIBER: Fiber is found in food such as vegetables, fruit, and cereal. Fibers act as "**brushes**" to clean the waste in the intestine.

MICROORGANISMS: Bacteria, mold, and yeast are microorganisms. They've been used for thousands of years to make **cheese**, yogurt, bread, and other foods.

MINERALS: Minerals are substances such as **calcium**, sodium, potassium, and iron. Your body needs minerals to help it work properly.

ORGANIC FOODS: Natural food products made without the use of chemical fertilizers and **pesticides** are called organic.

PROTEINS: Proteins are essential to help the body **grow**. They're found in meat, fish, eggs, and milk.

VITAMINS: Vitamins are found in foods we eat and are important to our health. Vitamins A, B, and C are found in fruit, vegetables, and whole grains.

9
I Don't Have Nine Lives!

After we said **GOOD-BYE** to Victoria, we went to Hercule's grandmother's house. Granny Ironwhiskers is an extraordinary rodent. She's **Ninety-six** years old and still manages the family's business that makes the famous **"Poirat yellow"** trench coats.

"It's so good to see you, Geronimo," she said, *wringing* my paw.

"You, too," I gasped, checking for broken bones. Granny Ironwhiskers has an **IRON** grip!

"Here, dear, this package is for you,"

she squeaked. She handed me a **yellow** box.

It was a beautiful yellow trench coat with my **INITIALS** embroidered inside.

"Thank you!" I said, touched.

Just then, I remembered that I forgotten to tell Hercule about the **contest** with Thea, so I filled him in.

"It's on Sunday at the **Flying Fur Aviation Academy**," I explained.

"**Chili cheese puffs!**" Hercule shouted. This was a chance to spend time with my sister that he was not expecting!

"It's just a contest," I told Hercule, but he

wasn't listening. The **dreamy** expression in his eyes said it all.

"Thea is such a **SMART** and beautiful rodent. Imagine, Stilton — if we got *married*, you and I would be related!" he mused.

I practically choked.

Don't get me wrong — I love Hercule. But he's very INTENSE. Every time he gets me involved in one of his crazy cases, I practically lose my fur! Yes, having Hercule as a brother-in-law would be too RISKY. I'm not a cat — I don't have nine lives!

I tried to talk some sense into Hercule, but he just kept **blabbering** and **blabbering** away about Thea. "How should I act at the contest? If I show her how good I am, and win, she might be **IMPRESSED**. Then again, I could let her win, but if she finds out, she might be annoyed. And if I lose, I'll look like a real **cheesebrain**," he muttered. "Maybe I should give her lots of compliments . . . or I can buy her lots of gourmet cheeses. I don't know! What do you think, Stilton?" he asked.

I had started drooling, thinking about **GOURMET** cheeses — I just love them, and of course my sister would share! But I didn't know if it would **Win** her over. So I gave Hercule the advice that my aunt Sweetfur always gives me.

"Don't worry about it so much. It doesn't

matter if you win or lose. And if you don't know how to act . . . *just be yourself*! It always works!"

That put a big **Smile** on Hercule's face. "Thank you, Geronimo!" he said.

Aunt Sweetfur

THAT SPECIAL
SOMEONE!

I got up on Sunday **morning** and headed to the Flying Fur Aviation Academy. Thea was waiting impatiently.

Finally, Hercule arrived.

"At last! I thought you were getting **cold paws**!" my sister teased.

THea's Plane

Hercule smiled so **wide** his jaw broke. Well, okay, his jaw didn't really break, but you get the idea. He had a huge smile. "May the best rodent win!" he said with a wink.

Then he jumped into the bananaplane and Thea jumped into her **pink** plane.

"Contestants, prepare for takeoff!" yelled the announcer.

I heard Hercule pump himself up for his flight by roaring his war cry:

"HERRCUUUULLLE POOOIIIRAAAATTT!"

HERCULE'S PLANE

The pink plane rose into the air as light as a **hummingbird**. Ooohs and aaahs filled the air as Thea performed one acrobatic trick after another. Yes, my sister knew how to pilot a plane with STYLE and grace!

In the meantime, Hercule's yellow bananaplane rose higher and higher. Where was he going? To the moon? Suddenly it reemerged with an incredible nosedive, loop-de-loop, and triple roll. The crowd went wild. The judges each raised their PADDLES.

"Scores for Thea Stilton."

"Nine!"
"Nine!"
"Nine!"
"Nine!"
"Nine!"

"Nine!"
"Nine!"
"Nine!"
"Nine!"
"Nine!"

"Now the score for Hercule Poirat."

"Ten!"
"Ten!"
"Ten!"
"Ten!"
"Ten!"
"Ten!"
"Ten!"
"Ten!"
"Ten!"
"Ten!"

Hercule's point average was ten out of ten!
He had won!

The pink plane DELICATELY touched

the ground, followed by the bananaplane.

The two pilots climbed out of their planes. Then they shook paws. "Congratulations! You were **amazing**!" Thea told Hercule. "Maybe I could learn some of those 𝕥𝕣𝕚𝕔𝕜𝕤 for next time. That was so much fun!"

Hercule beamed. "Thanks, Thea! You were **amazing**, too! You are always amazing!" he sighed, staring at her **dreamily**.

Right then, a group of photographers began taking their photo as they held paws. **Click! Click! Click!** And a TV newscaster announced, "Yes, folks, it's the two aces of aviation shaking paws in a noble example of sportsmousehip!"

When the cameras stopped 𝕗𝕝𝕒𝕤𝕙𝕚𝕟𝕘, Hercule held up a paw and squeaked, "Don't leave, everyone! I have one last trick to show you!"

Congratulations!

Thanks!

He jumped into his plane and roared away in a **ZIGZAG**. As he flew, I could hear him singing:

"Flying is special! Flying is fun!
When you are flying, you've already won!
So look at the clouds and at the breathtaking sun,
and if you are lucky, at that special someone!"

When you are flying, you've already won! So look at the clouds and at the breathtaking sun, and if you are lucky, at that special someone!

Flying is special! Flying is fun!

The plane made some peculiar loops . . .

The plane made some *peculiar* loops. What was Hercule trying to do? Then I understood. He had drawn a **heart** in the sky, dedicated to Thea!

At first I thought my sister would **roll** her eyes. She's usually not into cheesy romantic gestures. But to my surprise, she just **grinned**.

Who knows? Maybe, one day, Hercule and I really will become related . . .

That **NIGHT** I dreamed that Thea and Hercule got married.

Can you guess what they served at the reception?

Lots of **real cheese** and lots of **bananas**!

Geronimo's dream

Now check out this bonus
Mini Mystery story!
Join me in solving a whisker-licking-
good mystery. Find clues along with me
as you read. Together, we'll be
super-squeaky investigators!

THE MOUSE
HOAX

A STRANGE
LITTLE GIFT

It was a busy day at the office. The telephones wouldn't stop ringing!

"Hello?" I answered my **desk phone**.

"Mr. Stilton? It's Mitzy Mouserson. Remember me?"

"Yes?" I answered my **cell phone**.

"Stilton, it's Andrew Whitetail. About that manuscript . . ."

On top of the phone calls, every few minutes someone entered my office and I lost my TRAIN of thought. Oh, excuse me! I haven't introduced myself. My name is Stilton, *Geronimo Stilton*, and I am the publisher of *The Rodent's Gazette*, the most **famouse** newspaper on Mouse Island.

So, I was in my office when an **enoRMouse** package entered the room. A familiar snout poked out from behind it.

"**Happy birthday**, Stilton!" a voice shouted.

It was my friend Hercule Poirat, the famouse detective.

"Birthday?" I repeated. "But **TODAY** isn't my birthday!"

"Oh, well," Hercule replied as he placed the package on my desk. "You should take the day off anyway!"

"Oh, I can't," I told him. "I have a **LOT** to do today."

Hercule got **closer** to my desk.

"Yes, I see that," he said. "You're always here, working. You should get out more! A change would be good for you. Come with me to my **office**."

My whiskers trembled at just the thought of the flea-infested shack Hercule calls his office. He is a complete slob, and his office is a total disaster area!

"I'm sorry, I can't," I told him quickly. "I really have to finish this article."

Hercule sighed. "All right, Stilton. I'll go. But first open the **little** gift I got you. Aren't you even a little curious about what's inside?"

A REAL STINKER

Inside the package was a painting. It was no masterpiece. In fact, it looked like it had been painted by my little cousin **MESSY PAWS**, and he's just a baby! It was a real **stinker**!

In the lower right-hand corner were the painter's initials: P.M.

"Do you like it?" Hercule asked me.

"Er, yes, of course!" I replied. I didn't want to offend him. "But it's a bit . . . odd. Where did you get it?"

"A while ago, I met a rat who was down on his **luck**," Hercule replied. "He gave it to me in exchange for some BREAD and cheese. Isn't it great?"

At that moment, one of the new editors, **Katie Cheeseheart**, popped in.

"Are you ready for the ART EXHIBIT?" she asked. "Tonight is the opening, remember?"

THE INVITATION TO THE SHOW

Oh, for the love of cheese! I had completely forgotten about the art show opening of the great painter **PABLO MOUSEHASSO**.

"Petunia Pretty Paws called," Katie told me. "She and Bugsy Wugsy will be there."

Ah, Petunia Pretty Paws! She is the most fascinating rodent I know. I have a TEENY, tiny crush on her.

"You can bring guests," Katie reminded me.

"I'll come!" Hercule said eagerly.

I sighed. Hercule is a very good friend, but whenever he's around, I end up in a SEA of trouble.

"Well, er, actually . . . I promised Benjamin I would take him," I replied.

Right at that moment, my dear little nephew appeared.

"Hi, BENJAMIN!" I exclaimed.

"Hi, Uncle G!" Benjamin said as he gave me a **huge** hug. "Is Hercule coming with us to the show? How nice!"

Hercule winked at me, and we all left together.

A RATASTIC VILLA!

The show was in Master Mousehasso's house.

"This guy sure has a **ratastic** villa!" exclaimed Hercule.

"**Shhhhh!**" I quieted him. "Do you want them to kick us out?"

At that moment, I heard the sweetest voice behind me.

"Hi, G!"

It was Petunia Pretty Paws!

Then a little mouse with black **braids** jumped out at me and threw her arms around my neck — it was Bugsy, Petunia's

PABLO MOUSEHASSO'S VILLA

niece and Benjamin's **best friend**.

I let the ladies enter first and then I gave the *invitations* to the butler.

"Mr. Stilton!" the butler exclaimed. "What an HONOR. And are these other guests with you?"

"Yes, this is my **nephew** Benjamin," I replied. "And this, er, is the famouse investigator Hercule Poirat."

Hercule was busy WAVING his magnifying glass in the butler's face.

My snout turned **purple** with embarrassment, but the butler didn't TWITCH a whisker.

"Welcome," he said kindly. "Please CLIMB this main stairway. On the

second floor you will see the BUFFET.
Have a good evening!"

"Thank you!" I replied, trying to smile
through my embarrassment.

Hercule disappeared in the crowd.

I offered my arm to **Petunia**, and we climbed the main stairway that led to the second floor.

I was on cloud nine!

THE GREAT MOUSEHASSO

The main hall was full of people admiring the paintings that hung on the walls. In one corner, I saw a rodent surrounded by photographers and admirers. It was Master Mousehasso!

"I want to see if I can get a picture, too!" Bugsy said as she showed off her digital camera with pride. "Come with me, Benjamin!"

"Can I, Uncle G?" Benjamin squeaked.

"Of course, Benjamin!" I said.

I was finally alone with Petunia when Hercule suddenly appeared, speaking

loudly as he was snacking.

"But . . . *chomp* . . . that guy . . . *chomp, chomp* . . . I . . . *chomp* . . ."

"Hercule!" I scolded. "You shouldn't talk with your mouth **fULL**!"

He just laughed.

"While you fill your head with **art**, I fill my stomach with **food**!"

My snout turned **purple** with embarrassment.

He ignored me.

"Listen up, Stilton," Hercule *whispered*. "This Mousehasso guy — I've seen him before, but I can't **remember** where. I just might go over there and ask him."

And he **disappeared** again!

Petunia turned to me and smiled *sweetly*.

"Why don't we go and get something to eat?" she asked.

So we approached the **super-crowded** refreshment table.

I had just managed to get my paws on two Gorgonzola **tarts** when a rodent asked: "Do you like my work?"

TARTS AND COUNTESSES

The rodent stuck out his **PAW**.

"It's very nice to meet you," he said. "I am Master **PABLO MOUSEHASSO**."

"M-my name is Stilton, *Geronimo Stilton*," I stuttered. I could hardly believe I was speaking with a master artist! "I am —"

"Oh, I know who you are!" he replied with a smile. "And I want to offer you an exclusive **interview** for your newspaper. What do you say?"

"That sounds **FABUMOUSE**!" I exclaimed. "When can we do it?"

"Right away!" he said. "Just follow me into my studio. Naturally, your LOVELY girlfriend can come with us!"

My snout turned **purple** with embarrassment. I haven't yet had the courage to tell Petunia how I feel about her!

"Can our niece and nephew come, too?" Petunia asked.

"It would be a **pleasure** to meet them," Mousehasso replied.

Meanwhile, Hercule was approaching. I didn't want him to see us: Who knew what kind of mess Hercule would get me into!

But right as he was arriving, Mousehasso mumbled something and ran off.

"Taste this!" Hercule said as he shoved a tart into my mouth. The TART went down the wrong pipe, and I turned RED, then green, then as

I turned red ...

...then green ...

...then as white as mozzarella!

WHITE as mozzarella.

Hercule **HIT** me really hard on the back until I spit out the tart. It flew across the room, hitting **Countess Snobella** in the back of the neck.

"How rude!" she shrieked, smacking me with a **CANE**. "Oh, for the love of **bananas**!"

Hercule shouted. "Stilton, when will you learn to leave little old ladies alone?"

When she heard Hercule call her an old lady, Countess Snobella began **CHASING** after him instead. I sighed with **relief** and led Petunia out of the way.

AN EXCLUSIVE INTERVIEW

The butler approached me.

"Mr. Stilton, the **MASTER** is waiting for you," he said.

I called Benjamin and Bugsy Wugsy, and together we all went into the studio.

"Shall we begin?" the **artist** asked. "I only have a few minutes."

"Yes, of course," I replied. "So, how did you become such a success?"

"It wasn't easy," Master Mousehasso said. "In the beginning, I never had much money or enough to eat. Sometimes I had to give away my paintings in exchange

for a bit of **BREAD** and **cheese**!"

HOW strangE! That sentence sounded very familiar.

Mousehasso continued. "Because I remember my humble beginnings, I am organizing a charity **auction** of a few of my works the day after tomorrow. The proceeds will help young artists. I hope you can make it."

"Oh, yes," I replied. "It would be a great **HONOR**."

Master Mousehasso rang a bell, and the butler

appeared with two ENORMOUSE packages.

Mousehasso gave one to Petunia and one to me.

"Don't open them right away," he instructed us. "It's a surprise!"

"I don't know how to thank you," I said breathlessly.

"Oh, it's nothing!" he replied. "I look forward to seeing you at the auction."

What a scoop!

I couldn't wait to get back to my office to write my article.

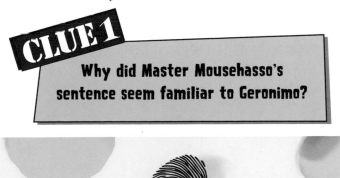

CLUE 1

Why did Master Mousehasso's sentence seem familiar to Geronimo?

THE MASTER'S GIFT

The next day, copies of *The Rodent's Gazette* flew off the stands. Bugsy's **photos** came out so well that I published one on the front page.

As I was enjoying my success, the phone **rang**.

It was Petunia Pretty Paws.

"Hi, G," she said sweetly. "There's a beautiful horse **GALLOPING** in my painting. What's yours like?"

For the love of cheese! I hadn't opened my gift from the master yet!

"I'll look right now," I told Petunia.

First I read the note:

I would have preferred to paint it in your office, but I wanted to surprise you!

Pablo Mousehasso

To:
Geronimo Stilton

Then I opened the package.

For the love of cheese! It was me!

"So, G?" Petunia asked. "What is it?"

My snout turned **purple** with embarrassment. It's a good thing Petunia couldn't see me.

"Er, well . . . it's a portrait of me," I replied.

"**Really?**" Petunia asked. "I'll come right over so I can see it. You don't mind, do you?"

Mind? I was on **cloud nine**!

I hung the **PAINTING** facing my desk, right next to the painting Hercule had given me.

Now this is a real masterpiece, I thought. *It's nothing like that* **stinker**!

Then the door to my office suddenly **BURST** open.

PABLO MOUSEHASSO

BREAD AND CHEESE

It was **Hercule Poirat**!

"Stilton!" he exclaimed. "I remembered where I've seen Mousehasso before! He was the rat who gave me the painting in exchange for some BREAD and cheese! He was such a TERRIBLE artist I don't know how he ever got famous!"

"Well, he isn't **TERRIBLE** anymore," I said. "Look what he gave me."

I pointed to the portrait hanging on the wall.

Hercule approached it with his magnifying glass.

"You put it right next to the stinker!"
he exclaimed. "Didn't you notice anything
STRANGE about these two paintings?"

Hercule was right — how had I
missed it?

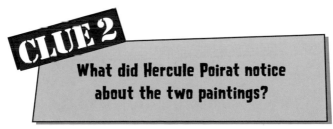

CLUE 2

**What did Hercule Poirat notice
about the two paintings?**

ARE YOU OKAY, G?

"The same mouse couldn't have painted **both** of these," I squeaked.

"It's quite a **mystery**," Hercule agreed.

At that moment, Bugsy, Benjamin, and Petunia Pretty Paws came in.

"Are you okay, G?" Petunia asked.

"I just made an important discovery," I told her. "**LOOK!** The **SIGNATURES** are similar. The initials in the corner of the painting Hercule gave me are the same as Pablo Mousehasso's!"

"Hey, *I* made the **DISCOVERY**!"

Hercule protested.

Bugsy picked up a slip of paper from the **ground** and handed it to me.

"This fell," she said.

"Thanks," I replied. It was the master's NOTE to me.

"**MOLDY MOZZARELLA!**" I exclaimed in surprise. "Look at this **strange** writing on the back of the note!"

I held it out for my friends to see.

THE ANAGRAM

"What does it mean?" Hercule asked.

"It's an ANAGRAM!" Petunia exclaimed.

"A **telegram**?" Hercule replied.

"No, an anagram." I explained, "It's a game in which the letters of a word are scrambled and need to be put back in order."

"Let's figure it out!"

Bugsy said. "The first group of letters is **YBU**. What does that mean?"

I thought and thought.

"Um, UBY?" I suggested. "YUB?"

"I'VE GOT IT!" Hercule shouted. "It spells BUY!"

"Nice work!" Benjamin and Bugsy exclaimed in **unison**. "Now we need to do the same thing with the other groups of letters to make a sentence."

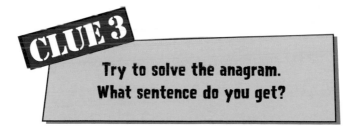

CLUE 3

**Try to solve the anagram.
What sentence do you get?**

YBU HTE
CLBAK
LTESRTE

THE CODED
MESSAGE

I was PERPLEXED. "What does 'buy the black letters' mean?"

"I don't think this sentence was written by the master," Benjamin pointed out. "The handwriting looks different."

"So someone else knew about the gift Master Mousehasso gave Uncle G," observed Bugsy. "And that mouse wrote a coded message to let Uncle G know —"

"To buy the black letters!" Benjamin finished with **excitement**.

"They must be for sale if Geronimo is supposed to buy them," Hercule **muttered**. "But who would be selling **BLACK LETTERS**?"

"I know!" exclaimed Petunia. "Tomorrow **morning** is Mousehasso's charity auction at his villa."

"Of course!" I agreed. "The master will be selling his **PAINTINGS** at the auction. Maybe the black letters will be for sale then!"

THE CHARITY AUCTION

When we arrived at the charity auction at Pablo Mousehasso's villa the next morning, the butler handed us a **catalog** of all the paintings that were for sale. Then we walked around to take a **look** at them.

"If you notice anything **strange**, let me know!" Hercule told us.

We stopped in front of a painting of a lake surrounded by **snowcapped** mountains.

"Do you see anything odd in this painting?" Bugsy Wugsy asked Hercule.

"Well, now that you mention it, yes I do," Hercule replied. "Those clouds remind me of a banana smoothie, and those mountains look a little like banana cakes!"

I rolled my eyes. Hercule LOVES

bananas the way most mice love cheese.

"Hey!" Benjamin whispered. "I see something **strange**. Look in the bottom right corner!"

"But of course!" Hercule exclaimed LOUDLY.

I didn't know what they were talking about. I didn't see anything but Master Mousehasso's **SIGNATURE**. But then I looked more closely.

BUT OF COURSE!

CLUE 4

What did Benjamin see in the painting?

🄰🄱🄲
THE BLACK LETTERS

There was a black letter in the white signature! It had to be one of the **BLACK LETTERS**. But where were the **others**?

We didn't have time to look because the auction was about to **start**.

"*Psst,*" Hercule whispered. "Let's look in the catalog and find the paintings with **BLACK** letters. WE'LL BUY aLL OF ThEM!"

Finding the paintings was easy: There were **five** of them!

"Soon we'll know what the author of the MYSTERIOUS note wanted to say!" Petunia said.

I had a sudden realization. "Who is going to PAY for all of these paintings?"

Benjamin gave me a pleading look.

"Won't **you**, Uncle?"

I could never say no to my **sweet** little nephew!

"Of course, Benjamin," I told him. "After all, there's a **mystery** to solve!"

Landscape
40" x 27"

Lower left:
**Still Life of Fruit
and Cheese**
20" x 35"

Lower right
Mousilda
27" x 43"

THe BlacK LetteRs

Light and Sea
50" x 25"

Red Flowers
50" x 25"

START YOUR BIDDING!

"Do you want some help bidding, Stilton?" Hercule asked.

"Oh, no!" I said.

"It's no problem," he replied. "I'll just offer an amount that's a little **TOO HIGH** to make sure we get the painting!"

"**Absolutely not!**" I insisted, twisting my whiskers anxiously. "I'll go **broke**!"

"Oh, fine." Hercule pouted. "Do it your way!"

The first few **PAINTINGS** were not the ones with the black letters. We watched the other rodents bid.

Holey cheese! The prices were so high I almost fainted.

"Why are they raising their paws, Uncle?" Benjamin asked.

"To show the price they are willing to pay," I replied. "Each raised paw means they are willing to pay **fifty dollars** more

than the previous rodent."

"WOW!" Benjamin exclaimed. "Those are some expensive paintings!"

Finally, the painting with the banana cake–shaped mountains came up.

"The opening price for this **splendid** painting is five hundred dollars," the auctioneer said. "Ladies and gentlemice, start your bidding!"

Five hundred dollars! I was about to faint from the price, but I raised my paw anyway.

"Five hundred **DOLLARS** to the

gentlemouse in the back!"

A lady rodent in the first row raised her hand.

"Five hundred fifty **DOLLARS** to the lady in front!"

Several more rodents raised their paws. Suddenly, a waiter came in with a huge tray of banana cream pastries.

Hercule waved his arms to get the **waiter's** attention: He really LOVES bananas! But every time he raised his arm, the auctioneer raised the price!

I tried to stop him, but Hercule continued lifting his arms until, finally, we got the painting for . . .

ONE THOUSAND DOLLARS!

ASTRONOMICAL PRICES

We still needed to buy **four** more paintings. And every time a **waiter** passed by with a tray of treats, Hercule raised his arm, **increasing** the price!

During bidding for the second painting, there was a tray of banana **muffins**.

I was going broke!

During bidding for the third painting, Hercule waved for the crispy banana chips.

SECOND PAINTING

THIRD PAINTING

FOURTH PAINTING

FIFTH PAINTING

I was really going broke!

During bidding for the fourth painting, the tray was full of banana sundaes.

I was really, really going broke!

During bidding for the fifth painting, I gave up.

I was completely broke!

But I was happy anyway. After all, the money was for a good cause!

ANOTHER
ANAGRAM

After the auction, we RETURNED to my house to study the **FIVE** paintings.

"So? Have you discovered anything?" asked Petunia.

"Well, the black letters are **L**, **M**, **E**, **H**, **P**, and **E**," Hercule replied.

"We knew that just by looking at the catalog!" said Benjamin.

"Yes, but we hadn't figured out that it was another kilogram!" explained Hercule.

"You mean another ANAGRAM," I told Hercule. "What do the letters spell?"

"Let's try rearranging them a few different ways," Benjamin suggested.

"H-E-E-L-M-P?" I suggested.

"M-E-E-P-H-L?" Bugsy tried.

HELP ME!

Hercule **nibbled** his way through **five** bananas and drank **two** banana smoothies as we worked.

"Maybe it's two words," Benjamin said. "Otherwise there are a lot of consonants."

"I figured it out!" Hercule shouted. "The letters spell **HELP ME**!"

"'Help me'?" I asked in astonishment. "Someone must be in **trouble**!"

"Who could it be?" asked Bugsy.

Hercule was so excited that he accidentally spilled his smoothie on one

of the paintings. The paint smeared
as he wiped it off.

"Look at this!" exclaimed Petunia.

A **hidden** picture had appeared.

"It's part of a **MAP**!" Bugsy realized.
"But it's **incomplete**."

"I think I know where the rest of the
map is," said Benjamin. "Hercule, can
you wipe off the other paintings?"

THE MAP

Hercule didn't need to be asked twice: He happily **spilled** the smoothie on all the paintings to reveal the **pieces** of the map. One of the paintings, however, didn't seem to have a part of the map. **How strange!**

Hercule inspected every inch of the canvas until he discovered an eight-digit **number** in the corner.

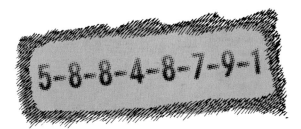

5-8-8-4-8-7-9-1

"What do these numbers mean?" Petunia asked.

"**I don't know**, but we'll figure it out!" Benjamin replied.

Meanwhile, Hercule put all the pieces of the map **TOGETHER**. The map's shape looked very familiar. I felt as though I had been to the place in the drawing. But **WHERE** was it?

Suddenly, Bugsy and **BENJAMIN**

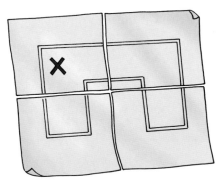

exclaimed in unison: "**We've got it!**"

"By my banana, I've got it, too!"

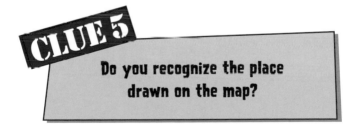

Hercule cried.

"**Me, too!**" added Petunia. "You recognize it, don't you, G?"

Suddenly, it came to me.

BUT OF COURSE!

CLUE 5

Do you recognize the place drawn on the map?

5-8-8-4-8-7-9-1

THE LAST PIECE OF THE PUZZLE

The mystery location on the map was Pablo Mousehasso's very own villa!

"WE DON'T HAVE A MINUTE TO SPARE!" Hercule exclaimed.

We hurried outside to a **TAXI**.

When we arrived at the villa, the

butler opened the door.

"The master is not at home," he told us. "He's at a ceremony receiving the RODENT OF THE YEAR award."

"That's perfect," I said. "We aren't here to see him anyway."

"Let's hurry!" Benjamin said as he slipped past the butler.

"Hey, wait a minute," **protested** the butler. "You can't just come in here!"

"You have to let us in," Bugsy insisted. "Someone's in trouble!"

The butler didn't know what to say. We just walked by him into the villa. Then we used the MAP to find the spot that was marked with an X.

We ended up in a small **STORAGE ROOM** in the cellar.

"Look, there's a **little door** down there!" exclaimed Bugsy.

We opened the door and found ourselves in front of a **WALL** made of bricks, some with markings numbering

them from **one** to nine.

Oh, for the love of cheese! We were so close to solving the mystery, but the wall was **blocking** us.

"I've got it!" Benjamin exclaimed suddenly. He *PULLED* the piece of canvas with the eight numbers from his pocket. Then he *pushed* on different bricks. The wall *moved* to reveal a secret passage. A small, skinny rodent appeared before our **eyes**.

"Finally you're here!" he said.

CLUE 6

How was Benjamin able to open the door to the secret passage?

SALVADOR RATI

The rodent explained the whole story.

"My name is **Salvador Rati**," he told us. "I met Pablo Mousehasso many years ago, when he was **KICKED OUT** of the New Mouse City **art school**. He was a charming mouse, but he didn't know what to do with a **PAINTBRUSH** between his paws! I, on the other hand, was talented but very shy. So he made me a proposal: I would create paintings that he would sign and sell, and we would split the profits."

"What a **cheater**!" Hercule exclaimed.

"My **PAINTINGS** did very well," Rati continued, "but Mousehasso was the one becoming FAMOUSE. He kept asking for more and more of the money. When I told him that I was tired of the lie, he locked me in his villa and forced me to work for FREE."

"That's awful!" Benjamin exclaimed.

The rest of us nodded in agreement.

"It's time to expose this HOAX," Hercule announced. "And I have a plan!"

RODENT OF
THE YEAR

We arrived just in time at the theater
where the RODENT OF THE YEAR
awards ceremony was being held. The
presentation had already begun.

Hercule disappeared backstage with
Rati while the rest of us sat in the last
row.

"And now, the moment you've all been waiting for: the RODENT OF THE YEAR award!" the emcee announced.

The **hostess** turned over the envelope.

"The most important rodent in New Mouse City this year is . . . **Salvador Rati**?!"

A **murmur** spread through the room.

I don't know how Hercule had done it, but he had managed to change the winner's name at the last **minute**!

Pablo Mousehasso stormed onstage, as **RED** as a tomato.

"Who dares to steal my *prize*?" he bellowed.

"I do!" Rati announced as he stepped onto the stage as well.

Mousehasso gasped.

"How did you manage to *escape*?" he asked. "Uh, I mean . . . who are you?"

"I'm a real **PAINTER**, not a con artist like you!" Rati said proudly.

"THAT'S NOT TRUE!" Mousehasso replied. "I'm a great painter!"

"Then prove it," Rati said calmly. "Right now, in front of everyone. You will **paint** my portrait, and I will **paint** yours!"

Mousehasso turned as pale as a slice of mozzarella, but there was no way around it. He had to agree to the challenge!

Rati, on the other paw, seemed very sure of himself as the emcee set up two easels and two canvases on the stage.

With trembling paws, Mousehasso began to paint. The crowd **murmured** softly.

This was the result:

PORTRAIT OF SALVADOR RATI
PAINTED BY PABLO MOUSEHASSO

Then it was Rati's turn. He picked up a brush and in a flash painted a *splendid* portrait of Mousehasso. The crowd broke out in **applause**.

PORTRAIT OF PABLO MOUSEHASSO
PAINTED BY SALVADOR RATI

THE TRUE STORY OF SALVADOR RATI

Salvador Rati was given the RODENT OF THE YEAR award, and Pablo Mousehasso went to jail, where he began taking a painting class.

The Rodent's Gazette published an exclusive story about Salvador Rati, and it was an enormouse success!

To celebrate, I invited all my friends to my house for a party. Rati was the guest of honor.

It was an unforgettable night!

YOU'RE THE INVESTIGATOR!

DID YOU FIGURE OUT THE CLUES?

1 **Why did Master Mousehasso's sentence seem familiar to Geronimo?**
Mousehasso said that in the past he had to exchange his paintings for bread and cheese. When Hercule gave Geronimo the bad painting, he told him he'd gotten it for bread and cheese. Hercule must have gotten it from Mousehasso!

2 **What did Hercule Poirat notice about the two paintings?**
The initials of the signatures on the two paintings are identical: *P.M.* and *Pablo Mousehasso.*

3 **Try to solve the anagram. What sentence do you get?**
The sentence is *Buy the black letters.*

4 **What did Benjamin see in the painting?**
He saw a black letter in the white signature.

5 **Did you recognize the place drawn on the map?**
It is Pablo Mousehasso's villa!

6 **How was Benjamin able to open the door to the secret passage?**
Benjamin pushed the numbered bricks in the sequence of the eight numbers on the canvas.

HOW MANY QUESTIONS DID YOU ANSWER CORRECTLY?

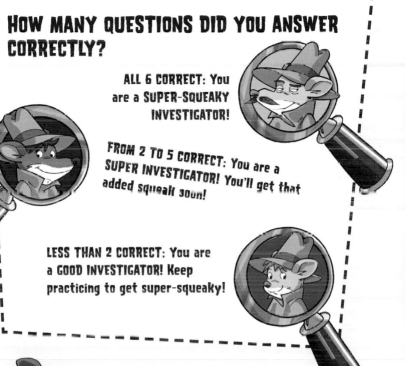

ALL 6 CORRECT: You are a SUPER-SQUEAKY INVESTIGATOR!

FROM 2 TO 5 CORRECT: You are a SUPER INVESTIGATOR! You'll get that added squeak soon!

LESS THAN 2 CORRECT: You are a GOOD INVESTIGATOR! Keep practicing to get super-squeaky!

Farewell until the next mystery!

Geronimo Stilton

GERONIMO'S JOKES

Now it's time for some fun and cheesy jokes to tickle your whiskers!

Q **What's a mouse's favorite game?**

A Hide and squeak!

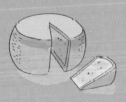

Q **What do you call cheese that isn't yours?**

A Nacho cheese!

Q **How does the barber get to work early?**

A He knows all the shortcuts!

Q **What was the shark's favorite number?**

A Ate!

Q Have you heard the joke about a mouse's dinner?

A Never mind — it's too cheesy!

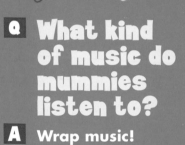

Q What kind of music do mummies listen to?

A Wrap music!

Q How do mice celebrate when they move into a new home?

A With a *mouse*warming party!

Q What do you call a mouse wearing earmuffs?

A Anything you want! He can't hear you.

Q Why did the skeleton go to the party alone?

A He had no body to go with him!

Q Why shouldn't you write with a broken pencil?

A Because it's pointless!

Q What do you call cheese that's sad?

A Blue cheese!

Q What do you call it when a dinosaur crashes his car?

A Tyrannosaurus wrecks!

Q **What do clouds wear under their shorts?**

A Thunderpants!

Q **What cheese surrounds a medieval castle?**

A *Moatzerella!*

Q **What do cats eat for breakfast?**

A Mice Krispies!

Q **What did one hat say to another?**

A "You stay here, I'll go on a head."

Be sure to read all my fabumouse adventures!

#1 Lost Treasure of the Emerald Eye

#2 The Curse of the Cheese Pyramid

#3 Cat and Mouse in a Haunted House

#4 I'm Too Fond of My Fur!

#5 Four Mice Deep in the Jungle

#6 Paws Off, Cheddarface!

#7 Red Pizzas for a Blue Count

#8 Attack of the Bandit Cats

#9 A Fabumouse Vacation for Geronimo

#10 All Because of a Cup of Coffee

#11 It's Halloween, You 'Fraidy Mouse!

#12 Merry Christmas, Geronimo!

#13 The Phantom of the Subway

#14 The Temple of the Ruby of Fire

#15 The Mona Mousa Code

#16 A Cheese-Colored Camper

#17 Watch Your Whiskers, Stilton!

#18 Shipwreck on the Pirate Islands

#19 My Name Is Stilton, Geronimo Stilton

#20 Surf's Up, Geronimo!

#21 The Wild, Wild West

#22 The Secret of Cacklefur Castle

A Christmas Tale

#23 Valentine's Day Disaster

#24 Field Trip to Niagara Falls

#25 The Search for Sunken Treasure

#26 The Mummy with No Name

#27 The Christmas Toy Factory

#28 Wedding Crasher

#29 Down and Out Down Under

#30 The Mouse Island Marathon

#31 The Mysterious Cheese Thief

Christmas Catastrophe

#32 Valley of the Giant Skeletons

#33 Geronimo and the Gold Medal Mystery

#34 Geronimo Stilton, Secret Agent

#35 A Very Merry Christmas

#36 Geronimo's Valentine

#37 The Race Across America

#38 A Fabumouse School Adventure

#39 Singing Sensation

#40 The Karate Mouse

#41 Mighty Mount Kilimanjaro

#42 The Peculiar Pumpkin Thief

#43 I'm Not a Supermouse!

#44 The Giant Diamond Robbery

#45 Save the White Whale!

#46 The Haunted Castle

#47 Run for the Hills, Geronimo!

#48 The Mystery in Venice

#49 The Way of the Samurai

#50 This Hotel Is Haunted!

#51 The Enormouse Pearl Heist

#52 Mouse in Space!

#53 Rumble in the Jungle

#54 Get into Gear, Stilton!

#55 The Golden Statue Plot

#56 Flight of the Red Bandit

The Hunt for the Golden Book

#57 The Stinky Cheese Vacation

#58 The Super Chef Contest

#59 Welcome to Moldy Manor

The Hunt for the Curious Cheese

#60 The Treasure of Easter Island

Join me and my friends as we travel through time in these very special editions!

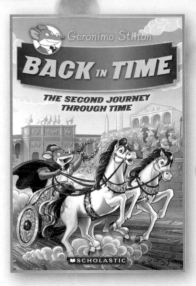

THE JOURNEY THROUGH TIME

BACK IN TIME:
THE SECOND JOURNEY THROUGH TIME

Don't miss these exciting Thea Sisters adventures!

Thea Stilton and the
Dragon's Code

Thea Stilton and the
Mountain of Fire

Thea Stilton and the
Ghost of the Shipwreck

Thea Stilton and the
Secret City

Thea Stilton and the
Mystery in Paris

Thea Stilton and the
Cherry Blossom Adventure

Thea Stilton and the
Star Castaways

Thea Stilton: Big Trouble
in the Big Apple

Thea Stilton and the
Ice Treasure

Thea Stilton and the
Secret of the Old Castle

Thea Stilton and the
Blue Scarab Hunt

Thea Stilton and the
Prince's Emerald

Thea Stilton and the Mystery
on the Orient Express

Thea Stilton and the
Dancing Shadows

Thea Stilton and the
Legend of the Fire Flowers

Thea Stilton and the
Spanish Dance Mission

Thea Stilton and the
Journey to the Lion's Den

Thea Stilton and the
Great Tulip Heist

Thea Stilton and the
Chocolate Sabotage

Thea Stilton and the
Missing Myth

Thea Stilton and the
Lost Letters

Be sure to read all my adventures in the Kingdom of Fantasy!

THE KINGDOM OF FANTASY

THE QUEST FOR PARADISE:
THE RETURN TO THE KINGDOM OF FANTASY

THE AMAZING VOYAGE:
THE THIRD ADVENTURE IN THE KINGDOM OF FANTASY

THE DRAGON PROPHECY:
THE FOURTH ADVENTURE IN THE KINGDOM OF FANTASY

THE VOLCANO OF FIRE:
THE FIFTH ADVENTURE IN THE KINGDOM OF FANTASY

THE SEARCH FOR TREASURE:
THE SIXTH ADVENTURE IN THE KINGDOM OF FANTASY

THE ENCHANTED CHARMS:
THE SEVENTH ADVENTURE IN THE KINGDOM OF FANTASY

Check out these very special editions featuring me and the Thea Sisters!

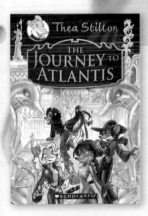

THE JOURNEY
TO ATLANTIS

THE SECRET OF
THE FAIRIES

THE SECRET OF
THE SNOW

MEET GERONIMO STILTONIX

He is a spacemouse — the Geronimo Stilton of a parallel universe! He is captain of the spaceship *MouseStar 1*. While flying through the cosmos, he visits distant planets and meets crazy aliens. His adventures are out of this world!

#1 Alien Escape

#2 You're Mine, Captain!

#3 Ice Planet Adventure

#4 The Galactic Goal

#5 Rescue Rebellion

Meet
GERONIMO STILTONOOT

He is a cavemouse — Geronimo Stilton's ancient ancestor! He runs the stone newspaper in the prehistoric village of Old Mouse City. From dealing with dinosaurs to dodging meteorites, his life in the Stone Age is full of adventure!

#1 The Stone of Fire

#2 Watch Your Tail!

#3 Help, I'm in Hot Lava!

#4 The Fast and the Frozen

#5 The Great Mouse Race

#6 Don't Wake the Dinosaur!

#7 I'm a Scaredy-Mouse!

#8 Surfing for Secrets

ABOUT THE AUTHOR

Born in New Mouse City, Mouse Island, **GERONIMO STILTON** is Rattus Emeritus of Mousomorphic Literature and of Neo-Ratonic Comparative Philosophy. For the past twenty years, he has been running *The Rodent's Gazette*, New Mouse City's most widely read daily newspaper.

Stilton was awarded the Ratitzer Prize for his scoops on *The Curse of the Cheese Pyramid* and *The Search for Sunken Treasure*. He has also received the Andersen 2000 Prize for Personality of the Year. One of his bestsellers won the 2002 eBook Award for world's best ratlings' electronic book. His works have been published all over the globe.

In his spare time, Mr. Stilton collects antique cheese rinds and plays golf. But what he most enjoys is telling stories to his nephew Benjamin.

1. Main entrance
2. Printing presses (where the books and newspaper are printed)
3. Accounts department
4. Editorial room (where the editors, illustrators, and designers work)
5. Geronimo Stilton's office
6. Helicopter landing pad

THE RODENT'S
GAZETTE

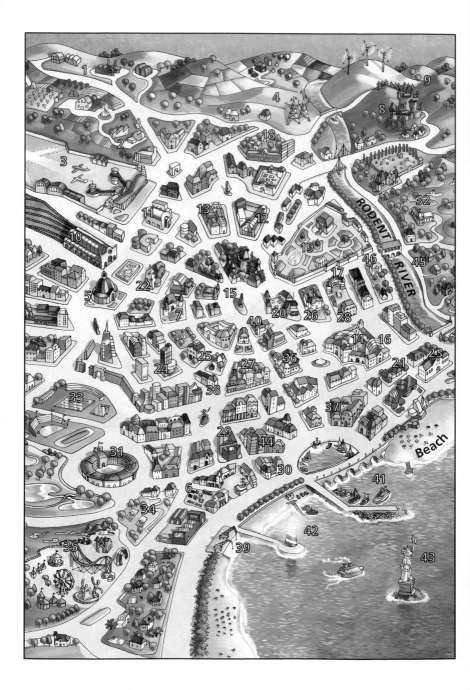

RODENT RIVER

Beach

Map of New Mouse City

Map of Mouse Island

1. Big Ice Lake
2. Frozen Fur Peak
3. Slipperyslopes Glacier
4. Coldcreeps Peak
5. Ratzikistan
6. Transratania
7. Mount Vamp
8. Roastedrat Volcano
9. Brimstone Lake
10. Poopedcat Pass
11. Stinko Peak
12. Dark Forest
13. Vain Vampires Valley
14. Goose Bumps Gorge
15. The Shadow Line Pass
16. Penny Pincher Castle
17. Nature Reserve Park
18. Las Ratayas Marinas
19. Fossil Forest
20. Lake Lake
21. Lake Lakelake
22. Lake Lakelakelake
23. Cheddar Crag
24. Cannycat Castle
25. Valley of the Giant Sequoia
26. Cheddar Springs
27. Sulfurous Swamp
28. Old Reliable Geyser
29. Vole Vale
30. Ravingrat Ravine
31. Gnat Marshes
32. Munster Highlands
33. Mousehara Desert
34. Oasis of the Sweaty Camel
35. Cabbagehead Hill
36. Rattytrap Jungle
37. Rio Mosquito

Dear mouse friends,
Thanks for reading, and farewell
till the next book.
It'll be another whisker-licking-good
adventure, and that's a promise!

Geronimo Stilton